THE KING OF THE MONKEYS ; THE STORY OF HOW A MONKEY BECAME A GOD

A CHINESE MYTHOLOGY

GOLU KUMAR

Contents

CHAPTER ONE

The Story of How a Monkey Became a God

The Hs Yu Chi

In dealing with the gods of China we noticed the monkey among them. Why
and in what manner he attained to that exalted rank is outlined in
the detail in the _Hsi yu chi_ [33]--a work the contents of which have
become woven into the fabric of Chinese legendary lore and are known
and loved by every intelligent native. Its pages are filled with
ghosts, demons, and fairies, good and bad, but "it contains no more
then the average Chinese believes to exist, and he believes in
such manifestations are so farmed that from the cradle to the grave he
lives and moves and has his being about them." Its characters
are said to be allegorical, though it may be doubted whether

these

implications may rightly be read into the Chinese text. Thus:

Hsüan (or Yüan) Chuang, or T'ang Sêng, is the pilgrim of the _Hsi yu

chi_, who symbolizes conscience, to which all actions are brought for

trial. The priestly garment of Hsüan Chuang symbolizes the good work

of the rectified human nature. It is held to be a great protection

to the new heart from the myriads of evil beings which surround it,

seeking its destruction.

Sun Hou-Tzu, the Monkey Fairy, represents human nature, which is prone

to all evil. His unreasonable vagaries moved Hsüan Chuang to compel

him to wear a Head-splitting Helmet which would contract upon his head

in moments of waywardness. The agonizing pressure thus caused would

bring him to his senses, irrespective of his distance from his master.

The iron wand of Sun Hou-Tzu is said to represent the use that can be

made of doctrine. It was useful for all purposes, great or small. By

a word it could be made invisible, and by a word it could become long

enough to span the distance between Heaven and earth.

Chu Pa-Chieh, the Pig Fairy, with his muck-rake, stands for the

coarser passions, which are constantly at war with the conscience in
their endeavors to cast off all restraint.

Sha Ho-Shang, Priest Sha, is a good representation of Mr. Faithful
in _The Pilgrim's Progress_. In the _Hsi yu chi_ he stands for the
human character, which is naturally weak and which needs constant
encouragement.

Hou-Sun Tzu's Legend

The deeds of this marvelous creature, the hero of the
Hsi yu chi,
are to be met with continually in Chinese popular literature, and they
are very much alive in the popular mind. In certain parts a regular
worship is offered to him, and in many temples representations of or
legends concerning him are to be seen or heard.

Other names by which Sun Hou-Tzu is referred to are Sun Hsing-chê,
Sun Wu-k'ung, Mei Hou-wang, Ch'i-t'ien Ta Shêng, and Pi-ma Wên, the
last-mentioned being a title which caused him annoyance by recalling
the derisive dignity conferred upon him by Yü Huang. [34] Throughout
the remainder of this chapter Sun Hou-tzu will be shortly referred
to as 'Sun.'

Beyond the seas, in the Eastern continent, in the kingdom of Ao-lai,
is the mountain, Hua-Kuo Shan. On the steep sides of this mountain, there
is a rocky point 36 feet 5 inches high and 24 feet in circumference. At
the very top an egg-formed, and, fructified by the breath of the wind,
gave birth to a stone monkey. The newly-born saluted the four points
of the horizon; from his eyes shone golden streaks of lightning,
which filled the palace of the North Pole Star with light. This light
subsided as soon as he was able to take nourishment.

"Today," said Yü Huang to himself, "I am going to complete the
wonderful diversity of the beings engendered by Heaven and earth. This
monkey will skip and gambol to the highest peaks of mountains, jump
about in the waters, and, eating the fruit of the trees, will be the
companion of the gibbon and the crane. Like the deer, he will pass
his nights on the mountain slopes, and during the day will be seen
leaping on their summits or in their caverns. That will be the finest
ornament of all for the mountains!"

The creature's exploits soon caused him to be proclaimed king
of the monkeys. He then began to try to find some means

of

becoming immortal. After traveling for eighteen years by land

and sea he met the Immortal P'u-the Tsu-Shih on the mountain

Ling-Tai-fang-tun. During his travels the monkey had gradually

acquired human attributes; his face remained always as it had been

originally, but dressed in human apparel he began to be civilized. His

new master gave him the family name of Sun and the personal name of

Wu-Kung, 'Discoverer of Secrets.' He taught him how to fly through

the air, and to change into seventy-two different forms. With one

leap he could cover 108,000 _li_ (about 36,000 miles).

A-Rod of Iron

Sun, after his return to Hua-Kuo Shan, slew the demon Hun-Shih Mo-wang,

who had been molesting the monkeys during his long absence. Then he

organized his subjects into a regular army, 47,000 all told. Thus the

peace of the simian kingdom was assured. As for himself, he could

not find a weapon to suit him and went to consult Ao Kuang, the

Lung Wang, or Dragon-king of the Eastern Sea, about it. It was from

him that he obtained the formidable rod of iron, formerly planted in the ocean by the Great Yü (Yü Wang) to regulate the level of the

waters. He pulled it out and modified it to suit his tastes. The

two extremities he bound round with gold bands, and on it engraved

the words: 'Gold-bound Wand of my Desires.' This magic weapon could

accommodate itself to all his wishes; being able to assume the most

incredible proportions or to reduce itself to the form of the finest of

needles, which he kept hidden in his ear. He terrorized the Four Kings

of the sea and dressed at their expense. The neighbouneighboringllied themselves with him. A splendid banquet with copious

libations of wine sealed the alliance of friendship with the seven

kings; but alas! Sun had partaken so liberally that when he was seeing

his guests off, no sooner had he taken a few steps than he fell into a

drunken sleep. The undertakers of Yen Wang, the King of the Hells, to

whom Lung Wang had accused him as the disturber of his watery kingdom,

seized his soul, put chains around its neck, and led it down to the

infernal regions. Sun awoke in front of the gate of the kingdom of

the dead, broke his fetters, killed his two custodians, and, armed with his magic staff, penetrated the realm of Yen Wang, where

he threatened to carry out general destruction. He called to the ten

infernal gods to bring him the Register of the Living and the Dead,

tore out with his hand the page on which were written his name

and those of his monkey subjects, and then told the King of the Hells

that he was no longer subject to the laws of death. Yen Wang yielded,

though with bad grace, and Sun returned triumphant from his expedition

beyond the tomb.

Before long Sun's escapades came to the knowledge of Yü Huang. Ao

Kuang and Yen Wang each sent deputies to the Master of Heaven, who

took note of the double accusation, and sent T'ai-PO Chin-hsing to

summon before him this disturber of the heavenly peace.

The Heavenly Stables' Grand Master

To keep him occupied, Sun was appointed Grand Master of the

Heavenly Stables, and was entrusted with the feeding of Yü Huang's

horses; his official celestial title being Pi-ma Wên. Later on, learning the object of the creation of this derisory appointment,

he overturned the Master's throne, seized his staff, broke down the

South Gate of Heaven, and descended on a cloud to Hua-
Kuo Shan.

The Heavenly Peach-Grand Garden's Superintendent
Yü Huang in great indignation organized a siege of Hua-
Kuo Shan,
but the Kings of Heaven and the generals with their
celestial armies
were repulsed several times. Sun now arrogated to himself
the pompous
title of Grand Saint, Governor of Heaven. He had this
emblazoned on
his banners and threatened Yü Huang that he would carry
destruction
into his kingdom if he refused to recognize his new dignity.
Yü
Huang, alarmed at the result of the military operations,
agreed to
the condition laid down by Sun. The latter was then
appointed Grand
Superintendent of the Heavenly Peach-garden, the fruit of
which
conferred immortality, and a new palace was built for him.

Immortality in two forms
Having made minute observations on the secret
properties of the
peaches, Sun ate of them and was thus assured against
death. The
time was ripe for him to indulge in his tricks without
restraint,
and an opportunity soon presented itself. Deeply hurt at
not having

been invited to the feast of the Peach Festival, P'an-to Hui, given

periodically to the Immortals by Wang-mu Niang-Niang, the Goddess of

the Immortals, he resolved upon revenge. When the preparations for the

feast were complete he cast a spell over the servants, causing them

to fall into a deep sleep, and then ate up all the juiciest meats

and drank the fine wines provided for the heavenly guests. Sun had,

however, indulged himself too liberally; with a heavy head and bleary

eye he missed the road back to his heavenly abode and came unaware

to the gate of Lao Chün, who was, however, absent from his palace. It

was only a matter of a few minutes for Sun to enter and swallow the

pills of immortality that Lao Chün kept in five gourds. Thus Sun,

doubly immortal, riding on the mist, again descended to Hua-Kuo Shan.

Sun Hou-Tzu Captured

These numerous misdeeds aroused the indignation of all the gods and

goddesses. Accusations poured in upon Yü Huang, and he ordered the Four

Gods of the Heavens and their chief generals to bring Sun to him. The

armies laid siege to Hua-Kuo Shan, a net was spread in the

heavens,

and fantastic battles took place, but the resistance of the enemy was as

strenuous and obstinate as before.

Lao Chün and Êrh-lang, nephew of Yü Huang, then appeared on the

scene. Sun's warriors resisted gallantly, but the forces of Heaven

were too much for them, and at length, they were overcome. At this

juncture, Sun changed his form, and despite the net in the sky

managed to find a way out. In vain search was made everywhere, until

Li T'ien-wang, by the help of his devil-finding mirror, detected the

quarry and informed Êrh-lang, who rushed off in pursuit. Lao Chün

hurled his magic ring on the tonto head of the fugitive, who stumbled

and fell. Quick as lightning, the celestial dog, T'ien Kou, who was

in Êrh-lang's service, threw himself on him, bit him in the calf,

and caused him to stumble afresh. This was the end of the fight. Sun,

surrounded, was seized and chained. The battle was won.

Sun escapes from Lao Chün's Furnace

The celestial armies now raised the siege and returned to their

quarters. But a new and unexpected difficulty arose. Yü Huang condemned

the criminal to death, but when they went to carry out the sentence
the executioners learned that he was invulnerable; swords, iron,
fire, and even lightning, could make no impression on his skin. Yü Huang,
alarmed, asked Lao Chün the reason for this. The latter replied that
nothing was surprising about it, seeing that the knave had
eaten the peaches of life in the garden of Heaven and the pills of
immortality that he had composed. "Hand him over to me," he added. "I
will distill him in my furnace of the Eight Trigrams, and extract from
his composition the elements which render him immortal."

Yü Huang ordered that the prisoner be handed over, and in the sight
of all, he was shut up in Lao Chün's alchemical furnace, which for
forty-nine days was heated white-hot. But at an unguarded moment
Sun lifted the lid, emerged in a rage, seized his magic staff, and
threatened to destroy Heaven and exterminate its inhabitants. Yü Huang,
at the end of his resources, summoned Buddha, who came and addressed
Sun as follows: "Why do you wish to possess yourself of the Kingdom
of the Heavens?"

"Have I not powerful enough to be the God of Heaven?" was the arrogant reply.

"What qualifications have you?" asked Buddha. "Enumerate them."

"My qualifications are innumerable," replied Sun. "I am invulnerable,

I am immortal, I can change myself into seventy-two different forms,

I can ride on the clouds of Heaven and pass through the air at will,

with one leap I can traverse a hundred and eight thousand _li_."

"Well," replied Buddha, "have a match with me; I wager that in one

leap you cannot even jump out of the palm of my hand. If you succeed

I will bestow upon you the sovereignty of Heaven."

Broad-jump Competition

Sun rose into space, flew like lightning in the great vastness, and

reached the confines of Heaven, opposite the five great red pillars

which are the boundaries of the created universe. On one of them

he wrote his name, as irrefutable evidence that he could reach this

extreme limit; this done, he returned triumphantly tthe o demand of Buddha

the coveted inheritance.

"But, wretch," said Buddha, "you never went out of my hand!"

"How is that?" rejoined Sun. "I went as far as the pillars of Heaven,

and even took the precaution of writing my name on one of them as
proof in case of need."

"Look then at the words you have written," said Buddha, lifting
a finger on which Sun read with stupefaction his name as he had
inscribed it.

Buddha then seized Sun, transported him out of Heaven, and changed
his five fingers into the five elements, metal, wood, water, fire,
and earth, which instantly formed five high mountains contiguous to
each other. The mountains were called Wu Hsing Shan, and Buddha shut
Sun up in them.

Conditions of Release
Thus subdued, Sun would not have been able to get out of his stone
prison but for the intercession of Kuan Yin P'u-sa, who obtained
his release on his solemn promise that he would serve as a guide,
philosopher, and friend to Hsüan Chuang, the priest who was to
undertake the difficult journey of 108,000 _li_ to the Western
Heaven. This promise, on the whole, he fulfilled in the service
of Hsüan Chuang during the fourteen years of the long journey. Now

faithful, now restive and undisciplined, he was always the one to

triumph in the end over the eighty-one fantastical tribulations which

beset them as they journeyed.

Sha Ho-Shang

One of the principals of Sun's fellow servants of the Master was

Sha Ho-Shang.

He is depicted wearing a necklace of skulls, the heads of the nine

Chinese deputies sent in former centuries to find the Buddhist canon,

but whom Sha Ho-Shang had devoured on the banks of Liu-Sha River when

they had attempted to cross it.

He is also known by the name of Sha Wu-ching and was originally

Grand Superintendent of the Manufactory of Stores for Yü Huang's

palace. During a great banquet given on the Peach Festival to all

the gods and Immortals of the Chinese Olympus, he let fall a crystal

bowl, which was smashed to atoms. Yü Huang caused him to be beaten

with eight hundred blows, drove him out of Heaven, and exiled him to

earth. He lived on the banks of the Liu-Sha Ho, where every seventh

day a mysterious sword appeared and wounded him in the neck. Having

no other means of subsistence, he used to devour the

passers-by.

Sha Ho-Shang becomes Baggage-coolie

When Kuan Yin passed through that region on her way to China to find

the priest who was predestined to devote himself to the laborious

the undertaking the quest for the sacred Buddhist books, Sha Ho-Shang

threw himself on his knees before her and begged her to put an end

to all his woes.

The goddess promised that he should be delivered by the priest,

her envoy, provided he would engage himself in the service of the

pilgrim. On his promising to do this, and to lead a better life,

she ordained him a priest. In the end, it came about that Hsüan

Chuang, when passing the Sha Ho, took him into his suite as coolie

to carry his baggage. Yü Huang pardoned him in consideration of the

service he was rendering to the Buddhist cause.

Chu Pa-chieh

Chu Pa-chieh is a grotesque, even gross, personage, with all the

instincts of animalism. One day, while he was occupying the high office

of the Overseer-general of the Navigation of the Milky Way, he, during a

fit of drunkenness, vilely assaulted the daughter of Yü Huang. The
latter had him beaten with two thousand blows from an iron hammer,
and exiled to earth to be reincarnated.

During his transition, a mistake was made, and entering the womb of
a sow he was born half-man, half-pig, with the head and ears of a
pig and a human body. He began by killing and eating his mother, and
then devoured his little porcine brothers. Then he went to live on the
wild mountain Fu-ling Shan, where, armed with an iron rake, he first
robbed and then ate the travelers who passed through that region.

Mao Êrh-chieh, who lived in the cave Yün-chan Tung, engaged him as
a carrier of her personal effects, which she afterward bequeathed to him.

Yielding to the exhortations of the Goddess Kuan Yin, who, at the
time of her journey to China, persuaded him to lead a less dissolute
life, he was ordained a priest by the goddess herself, who gave him
the name of Chu (Pig), and the religious name of Wu-nêng, 'Seeker
after Strength.' This monster was knocked down by Sun when the latter
was passing over the mountain accompanied by Hsüan Chuang, and he

declared himself a disciple of the pilgrim priest. He accompanied him

throughout the journey and was also received in the Western Paradise

as a reward for his aid to the Buddhist propaganda.

Hsüan Chuang, the Master

The origin of this priest was as follows: In the reign of the Emperor

T'ai Tsung of the T'ang dynasty, Ch'ên Kuang-jui, a graduate of Hai

Chou, in his examination for the doctor's degree, came out as _chuang

yüan_, first on the list. Wên Chiao (also named Manthang Chiao), the

daughter of the minister Yin K'ai-shan, met the young academician,

fell in love with him, and married him. Several days after the wedding

the Emperor appointed Ch'ên Kuang-jui Governor of Chiang Chou (modern

Chên-chiang Fu), in Kiangsu. After a short visit to his native town, he

started to take up his post. His old mother and his wife accompanied

him. When they reached Hung Chou his mother fell sick and they were

forced to stay for a time at the Inn of Ten Thousand Flowers, kept

by one Liu Hsiao-êrh. Days passed; the sickness did not leave her,

and as the time for her son to take over the seals of office was

drawing near, he had to proceed without her.

The Released Carp

Before his departure he noticed a fisherman holding in his hand a fine

carp; this he bought for a small sum to give to his mother. Suddenly

he noticed that the fish had a very extraordinary look, and, changing

his mind, he let it go in the waters of the Hung Chiang, afterward

telling his mother what he had done. She congratulated him on his

action and assured him that the good deed would not go unrewarded.

The Chuang Yüan Murdered

Ch'ên Kuang-jui re-entered his boat with his wife and a servant. They

were stopped by the chief waterman, Liu Hung, and his assistant. Struck

by the great beauty of Ch'ên Kuang-juJui'sife, the former planned

a crime which he carried out with the help of his assistant. In the

dead of night, he took the boat to a retired spot, killed Ch'ên and

his servant, threw their bodies into the river, seized his official

documents of title and the woman he coveted, passed himself off as the

real _chuang yüan_, and took possession of the magistracy of Chiang

Chou. The widow, who was with child, had two

alternatives--silence

or death. Meantime she chose the former. Before she gave birth to her

child, T'ai-PO Chin-hsing, the Spirit of the South Pole Star, appeared

to her and said he had been sent by Kuan Yin, the Goddess of Mercy,

to present her with a son whose fame would fill the Empire. "Above

all," he added, "take every precaution lest Liu Hung kill the child,

for he will certainly do so if he can." When the child was born the

mother, during the absence of Liu Hung, determined to expose it rather

than see it slain. Accordingly, she wrapped it up carefully in a shirt

and carried it to the bank of the Blue River. She then bit her finger,

and with the blood wrote a short note stating the child's origin,

and hid it in its breast. Moreover, she bit off the infant's left little toe, like an indelible mark of identity. No sooner had this been

done than a gust of wind blew a large plank to the river's edge. The

poor mother tied her infant firmly to this plank and abandoned it to

the mercy of the waves. The waif was carried to the shore of the isle

of Chin Shan, on which stands the famous monastery of Chin-shan Ssu,

near Chinkiang. The cries of the infant attracted the

attention of

an old monk named Chang Lao, who rescued it and gave it the name of

Chiang Liu, 'Waif of the River.' He reared it with much care and

treasured the note its mother had written with her blood. The child

grew up, and Chang Lao made him a priest, naming him Hsüan Chuang on

the day of his taking the vows. When he was eighteen years of age,

having one day quarreled with another priest, who had cursed him and

reproached him for having neither father nor mother, he, much hurt,

went to his protector Chang Lao. The latter said to him: "The time has

come to reveal to you your origin." He then told him all, showed him

the note and made him promise to avenge his assassinated father. To

this end, he was made a roving priest, went to the official Court,

and eventually got into touch with his mother, who was still living

with the prefect Liu Hung. The letter placed in his bosom, and the

shirt in which he had been wrapped, easily proved the truth of his

statements. The mother, happy at having found her son, promised to

go and see him at Chin Shan. To do this, she pretended to be sick, and to Liu Hung that formerly, when still young, she had

taken a vow that she had not yet been able to fulfill. Liu Hung himself

helped her to do so by sending a large gift of money to the priests

and allowing her to go with her servants to perform her devotions at

Chin-shan Su. On this second visit, during which she could speak

more freely with her son, she wished to see for herself the wound

she had made on his foot. This removed the last shadow of a doubt.

Hsüan Chuang finds his Grandmother

She told Hsüan Chuang that he must, first all, go to Hung Chou and

find his grandmother, formerly left at the Inn of Ten Thousand Flowers,

and then on to Ch'ang-an to take to her father Yin K'ai-shan a letter,

putting him in possession of the chief facts concerning Liu Hung,

and praying to him to avenge her.

She gave him a stick of incense to take to her mother-in-law. The old

lady lived the life of a beggar in a wretched hovel near the city gate

and had become blind from weeping. The priest told her of the tragic

death of her son, then touched her eyes with the stick of incense, and

her sight was restored. "And I," she exclaimed, "have so

often accused

my son of ingratitude, believing him to be still alive!" He took her

back to the Inn of Ten Thousand Flowers and settled the account, then

hastened to the palace of Yin K'ai-shan. Having obtained an audience,

he showed the minister the letter and informed him of all that had

taken place.

The Murderer Executed

The following day a report was presented to the Emperor, who gave

orders for the immediate arrest and execution of the murderer of

Ch'ên Kuang-jui.

Yin K'ai-shan went with all haste to Chên-Chiang, where he arrived

during the night, surrounded the official residence, and seized

the culprit, whom he sent to the place where he had committed the

murder. His heart and liver were torn out and sacrificed to the victim.

The Carp's Gratitude

Now it happened that Ch'ên Kuang-jui was not dead after all. The

carp released by him was no other than Lung Wang, the God

of the River, who had been going through his kingdom in that guise and had been caught in the fisherman's net. On learning that his

rescuer had been cast into the river, Lung Wang had saved him and

appointed him an officer of his Court. On that day, when his son,

wife, and father-in-law were sacrificing the heart of his assassin

to his _manes_ on the riverbank, Lung Wang ordered that he return

to earth. His body suddenly appeared on the surface of the water,

floated to the bank, revived, and came out full of life and health. The

happiness of the family reunited under such unexpected circumstances

may well be imagined. Ch'ên Kuang-jui returned with his father-in-law

to Chên-Chiang, where he took up his official post, eighteen years

after his nomination to it.

Hsüan Chuang became the Emperor's favorite priest. He was held in

great respect at the capital, and had innumerable honors bestowed upon

him, and in the end was chosen for the journey to the Western Paradise,

where Buddha in person handed him the sacred books of Buddhism.

Pai Ma, the White Horse

When he left the capital, Hsüan Chuang had been presented by the

Emperor with a white horse to carry him on his long pilgrimage. One

day, when he reached Shê-plan Shan, near a torrent, a dragon emerged

from the deep riverbed and devoured both the horse and its saddle. Sun

tried in vain to find the dragon, and at last, had to seek the aid of

Kuan Yin.

Now Yü Lung San T'ai-Tzu, son of Ao Jun, Dragonking of the Western

Sea, having burnt a precious pearl on the roof of his father's palace,

was denounced to Yü Huang, who had him beaten with three hundred blows

and suspended in the air. He was awaiting death when Kuan Yin passed

on her way to China. The unfortunate dragon requested the goddess

to pity him, whereupon she prevailed upon Yü Huang to spare

his life on the condition that he served as a steed for her pilgrim on the

expedition to the Western Paradise. The dragon was handed over to

Kuan Yin showed him the deep pool in which he was to dwell while

awaiting the arrival of the priest. It was this dragon who had devoured

Hsüan Chuang's horse and Kuan Yin now bade him change himself into a

horse of the same color to carry the priest to his destination. He

had the honor of bearing on his back the sacred books that Buddha
gave to T'ai Tsung's deputy, and the first Buddhist temple built at
the capital bore the name of Pai-ma Miao, 'Temple of the White Horse.'

Perils by the Way
   It is natural to expect that numberless exciting adventures should
befall such an interesting quartette, and indeed the _Hsi yu chi_,
which contains a hundred chapters, is full of them. The pilgrims
encountered eighty difficulties on the journey out and one on the
journey home. The following examples are characteristic of the rest.

The Grove of Cypress-trees
   The travelers were making their way westward through shining
waters and over green hills, where they found endless luxuriance
of vegetation and flowers of all colors in profusion. But the way
was long and lonely, and as darkness came on without any sign of
habitation the Priest said: "Where shall we find a resting-place for
the night?" The Monkey replied: "My Master, he who has left home
and become a priest must dine on the wind and lodge on

the water,
lie down under the moon and sleep in the forest; everywhere is his
home; why then ask where shall we rest?" But Pa-chieh, who was the
bearer of the pilgrim's baggage was not satisfied with this reply,
and tried to get his load transferred to the horse, but was silenced
when told that the latter's sole duty was to carry the Master.

However, the Monkey gave Pai Ma a blow with his rod, causing him to
start forward at a great pace, and in a few minutes from the brow of
a hill, Hsüan Chuang espied in the distance a grove of cypress trees,
beneath the shade of which was a large enclosure. This seemed a
suitable place to pass the night, so they made toward it, and as
they approached observed in the enclosure a spacious and luxurious
establishment. There being no indications that the place was then
inhabited, the Monkey made his way inside.

A Proposal of Marriage
He was met by a lady of charming appearance, who came out of an inner
room, and said: "Who is this that ventures to intrude upon a widow's
household?" The situation was embarrassing, but the lady proved to

be most affable, welcomed them all very heartily, told them how she

became a widow and had been left in possession of riches in abundance,

and that she had three daughters, Truth, Love, and Pity by name. She

then proceeded to propose marriage, not only on behalf of herself, but her three daughters as well. They were four men,

and there were four women; she had mountain lands for fruit trees,

dry lands for grain, flooded fields for rice--more than five thousand

acres of each; horses, oxen, sheep, pigs innumerable; sixty or seventy

farmsteads; granaries choked with grain; storehouses full of silks

and satins; gold and silver enough to last several lifetimes however

extravagantly they lived. Why should the four travelers not finish

their journey there, and be happy ever afterward? The temptation was

great, especially as the three daughters were ladies of surpassing

beauty as well as adepts at needlework and embroidery, well-read,

and able to sing sweetly.

But Hsüan Chuang sat as if listening to frogs after rain, unmoved

except by anger that she should attempt to divert him from his heavenly

purpose, and in the end the lady retired in a rage, slamming

the door
behind her.

The covetous Pa-chieh, however, expressed himself in favor of
accepting the widow's terms. Finding it impossible to do so openly,
he stole round to the back and secured a private interview. His
appearance was against him, but the widow was not altogether
uncompliant. She not only entertained the travellertavelerseed
to Pa-cChiehretiring within the household in the character of a
son-in-law, the other three remaining as guests in the guest rooms.

Blind Man's Buff

But a new problem now arose. If Pa-chieh were wedded to one of the
three daughters, the others would feel aggrieved. So the widow proposed
to blindfold him with a handkerchief and marry him to whichever
he succeeded in catching. But, with the bandage tied over his eyes,
Pa-chieh only found himself groping in darkness. "The tinkling sound
of female trinkets was all around him, and the odor of musk was in his
nostrils; like fairy forms, they fluttered about him, but he could no
more grasp one than he could a shadow. One way and

another he ran till
he was too giddy to stand, and could only stumble
helplessly about."

The prospective mother-in-law then unloosed the
bandage and informed
Pa-chieh that it was not her daughters' 'slipperiness,' as he
had
called it, which prevented their capture, but the extreme
modesty of
each in being generous enough to forgo her claims in favor
of one of
her sisters. Pa-chieh thereupon became very importunate,
urging his
suit for any one of the daughters or the mother herself or
all
three or all four. This was beyond all conscience, but the
widow was
equal to the emergency and suggested another solution.
Each of her
daughters wore a waistcoat embroidered in jewels and gold.
Pa-chieh
was to try these on in turn, and to marry the owner of the
one which
fitted him. Pa-chieh put one on, but as he was tying the cord
around
his waist it transformed itself into strong coils of rope that
bound
him tightly in every limb. He rolled about in excruciating
agony,
and as he did so the curtain of enchantment fell and the
beauties
and the palace disappeared.

The next morning the rest of the party on waking up also found that all

had changed, and saw that they had been sleeping on the ground in the

cypress grove. On searching they found Pa-Chieh bound fast to a

tree. They cut him down, to pursue the journey of a sadder and wiser Pig

and the butt of many a quip from his fellow travelers.

The Lotus Cave

When the party left the Elephant Country, seeing a mountain ahead,

the Master warned his disciples to be careful. Sun said: "Master, say

not so; remember the text of the Sacred Book, 'So long as the heart is

right there is nothing to fear.'" After this Sun kept a close watch

on Pa-chieh, who, while professing to be on guard, slept most of the

time. When they arrived at Ping-ting Shan they were approached by a

woodcutter, who warned them that in the mountain, which extended for

600 _li_ (200 miles), there was a Lotus Cave, inhabited by a band

of demons under two chiefs, who were lying in wait to devour the

travelers. The woodcutter then disappeared. Accordingly, Pa-chieh

was ordered to keep watch. But, seeing some hay, he lay down and went to sleep, and the mountain demons carried him away to the Lotus Cave.

On seeing Pa-chieh, the second chief said: "He is no good; you must
go in search of the Master and the Monkey." All this time the Monkey,
to protect his Master was walking ahead of the horse, swinging his
club up and down and to right and left. The Demon-king saw him from
the top of the mountain and said to himself: "This Monkey is famous
for his magic, but I will prove that he is no match for me; I will
yet feast on his Master." So, descending the mountain, he transformed
himself into a lame beggar and waited by the roadside. The Master,
out of pity, persuaded the Monkey to carry him. While on the Monkey's
back the Demon, by magic skill, threw Mount Mêru onto Sun's head,
but the Monkey warded it off with his left shoulder and walked
on. Then the Demon threw Mount Ô-mei onto Sun's head, and this
he warded off with his right shoulder, and walked on, much to the
Demon's surprise. Lastly, the Demon caused T'ai Shan to fall onto his
head. This at last stunned the Monkey. Sha Ho-sShangnow defended the
Master with his staff, which was, however, no match for the

Demon's

starry sword. The Demon seized the Master and carried him under one

arm and Sha Ho-Shang under the other to the Lotus Cave.

The two Demons then planned to take their two most precious things,

a yellow gourd and a jade vase, and try to bottle the Monkey. They

arranged to carry them upside down and call out the Monkey's name. If

he replied, then he would be inside, and they could seal him up,

using the seal of the great Ancient of Days, the dweller in the

mansion of T'ai Sui. [35]

The Monkey under the Mountain

When the Monkey found that he was being crushed under the mountain he

was greatly distressed about his Master, and cried out: "Oh, Master,

you delivered me from under the mountain before, and trained me in

religion; how is it that you have brought me to this pass? If you

must die, why should Sha Ho-Shang and Pa-chieh and the Dragon-horse

also, suffer?" Then his tears poured down like rain.

The spirits of the mountain were astonished at hearing these words. The

guardian angels of the Five Religions asked: "Whose is this mountain,

and who is crushed beneath it?" The local gods replied:

"The mountain
is ours, but who is under it we do not know." "If you do not know,"
the angels replied, "we will tell you. It is the Great Holy One,
the Equal of Heaven, who rebelled there five hundred years ago. He
is now converted and is the disciple of the Chinese ambassador. How
dare you lend your mountain to the Demon for such a purpose?" The
guardian angels and local gods then recited some prayers, and the
mountain was removed. The Monkey sprang up, brandishing his spear,
and the spirits at once apologized, saying that they were under
enforced service to the Demons.

While they were speaking Sun saw a light approaching, and asked
what it was. The spirits replied: "This light comes from the Demons'
magic treasures. We fear they are bringing them to catch you." Sun
then said: "Now we shall have some sport. Who is the Demon-chief's
associate?" "He is a Taoist," they replied, "who is always occupied in
preparing chemicals." The Monkey said: "Leave me, and I will catch them
myself." He then transformed himself into a duplicate of the Taoist.

The Magic Gourd

Sun went to meet the Demons, and in conversation learned from them that

they were on their way to catch the famous Monkey and that the magic

gourd and vase were for that purpose. They showed these treasures to

him and explained that the gourd, though small, could hold a thousand

people. "That is nothing," replied Sun. "I have a gourd which can

contain all the heavens." At this, they marveled greatly, and made a

bargain with him, according to which he was to give them his gourd,

after it had been tested as to its capacity to contain the heavens,

in exchange for their precious gourd and vase. Going up to Heaven,

the Monkey obtained permission to extinguish the light of the sun,

moon, and stars for one hour. At noon the next day, there was complete

darkness, and the Demons believed Sun when he stated that he had put

the whole heavens into his gourd so that there could be no light. They

then handed over to the Monkey their magic gourd and vase, and in

exchange, he gave them his false gourd.

The Magic Rope

On discovering that they had been deceived, the Demons made a complaint
to their chiefs, who informed them that Sun, by pretending to be one
of the Immortals, had outwitted them. They had now lost two out of
their five magic treasures. There remained three, the magic sword,
the magic palm fan, and the magic rope. "Go," said they, "and invite
our dear grandmother to come and dine on human flesh." Personating
one of the Demons, Sun himself went on this errand. He told the old
lady that he wanted her to bring with her the magic rope, with which
to catch Sun. She was delighted and set out in her chair carried by
two fairies.

When they had gone some few _li_, Sun killed the ladies, and then saw
that they were foxes. He took the magic rope, and thus had three of
the magic treasures. Having changed the dead so that they looked like
living creatures, he returned to the Lotus Cave. Many small demons came
running up, saying that the old lady had been slain. The Demon-king,
alarmed, proposed to release the whole party. But his younger brother
said: "No, let me fight Sun. If I win, we can eat them; if I fail,
we can let them go."

After thirty bouts Sun lost the magic rope, and the Demon lassoed him
with it and carried him to the cave, and took back the magic gourd
and vase. Sun now transformed himself into two false demons. One he
placed instead of himself in the lasso bound to a pillar, and then
went and reported to the second Demon-chief that Sun was struggling
hard and that he should be bound with a stronger rope lest he makes his escape. Thus, by this strategy, Sun obtained possession of the
magic rope again. By a similar trick, he also got back the magic gourd
and vase.

The Master Rescued

Sun and the Demons now began to wrangle about the respective merits
of their gourds, which, each assured the other, could imprison men
and make them obey their wishes. Finally, Sun succeeded in putting
one of the Demons into his gourd.

There ensued another fight concerning the magic sword and palm fan,
during which the fan was burnt to ashes. After more encounters, Sun
succeeded in bottling the second Demon in the magic vase and sealed
him up with the seal of the Ancient of Days. Then the magic sword
was delivered, and the Demons submitted. Sun returned to

the cave,

fetched his Master out, swept the cave clean of all evil spirits, and

they then started again on their westward journey. On the road, they

met a blind man, who addressed them saying: "Whither away, Buddhist

Priest? I am the Ancient of Days. Give me back my magic treasures. In

the gour,d I keep the pills of immortality. In the vase, I keep the

water of life. The sword I use to subdue demons. With the fan, I stir

up enthusiasm. With the cord, I bind bundles. One of these two Demons

had charge of the gold crucible. They stole my magic treasures and

fled to the mundane sphere of mortals. You, having captured them,

are deserving of great reward." But Sun replied: "You should be

severely punished for allowing your servants to do this evil in the

world." The Ancient of Days replied: "No, without these trials your

Master and his disciples could never attain perfection."

Sun understood and said: "Since you have come in person for the magic

treasures, I return them to you." After receiving them, the Ancient

of Days returned to his T'ai Sui mansion in the skies.

The Red Child Demon

By the autumn the travelers arrived at a great mountain. They saw
on the road a red cloud which the Monkey thought must be a demon. It
was a demon child who, to the Master, had had
himself bound and tied to the branch of a tree. The child repeatedly
cried out to the passers-by to deliver him. Sun suspected that it was
a trick, but the Master could no longer endure the pitiful wails; he
ordered his disciples to lose the child, and the Monkey to carry him.

As they proceeded on their way the Demon caused a strong whirlwind to
spring up, and during this, he carried off the Master. Sun discovered
that the Demon was an old friend of his, who, centuries before, had
pledged himself to eternal friendship. So he consoled his comrades
by saying that he felt sure no harm would come to the Master.

A Prospective Feast

Soon Sun and his companions reached a mountain covered with
pine forests. Here they found the Demon in his cave, intent upon
feasting on the Priest. The Demon refused to recognize his ancient
friendship with Sun, so the two came to blows. The Demon set fire to

everything so that the Monkey might be blinded by the smoke. Thus
he was unable to find his Master. In despair, he said: "I must get
the help of someone more skillful than myself." Pa-chieh was sent
to fetch Kuan Yin. The Demon then seized a magic bag, transformed
himself into the shape of Kuan Yin, and invited Pa-chieh to enter the
cave. The simpleton fell into the trap and was seized and placed in
the bag. Then the Demon appeared in his true form and said: "I am
the beggar child, and mean to cook you for my dinner. A fine man to
protect his Master you are!" The Demon then summoned six of his most
doughty generals and ordered them to accompany him to fetch his father,
King Ox-head, to dine off the pilgrim. When they had gone Sun opened
the bag, released Pa-chieh, and both followed the six generals.

The Generals Tricked

Sun thought that as the Demon had played a trick on Pa-chieh, he
would play one on his generals. So he hurried on in front of them
and changed himself into the form of King Oxhead. The Demon and
his generals were invited into his presence, and Red Child

said:

"If anyone eats of the pilgrim's flesh, his life will be prolonged

indefinitely. Now he is caught and I invite you to feast on him." Sun,

personifying the father, said: "No, I cannot come. I am fasting

today. Moreover, Sun has charge of the pilgrim, and if any harm befalls

him it will be the worse for you, for he has seventy-two magic arts. He

can make himself so big that your cave cannot contain him, and he

can make himself as small as a fly, a mosquito, a bee, or a butterfly."

Sun then went to Kuan Yin and appealed for help. She gave him a

bottle, but he found he could not move it. "No," said Kuan Yin,

"for all the forces of the ocean are stored in it."

Kuan Yin lifted it with ease and said: "This dew water is different

from dragon water, and can extinguish the fire of passion. I will

send a fairy with you on your boat. You need no sails. The fairy

needs only to blow a little, and the boat moves along without any

effort." Finally, the Red Child, having been overcome, repented and

begged to be received as a disciple. Kuan Yin received him and blessed

him, giving him the name of Steward.

The Demons of Blackwater River

One day the Master suddenly exclaimed: "What is that noise?" Sun

replied: "You are afraid; you have forgotten the Heart Prayer,

according to which we are to be indifferent to all the calls of the

six senses--the eye, ear, nose, tongue, body, mind. These are the Six

Thieves. If you cannot suppress them, how do you expect to see the

Great Lord?" The Master thought a while and then said: "O disciple,

when shall we see the Incarnate Model (Ju Lai) face to face?"

Pa-chieh said: "If we are to meet such demons as these, it will take

us a thousand years to get to the West." But Sha Ho-Shang rejoined:

"Both you and I are stupid; if we persevere and travel on, shoulder

to shoulder, we shall reach there at last." While thus talking, they saw before them a dark river in flood, which the horse could not

cross. Seeing a small boat, the Master said: "Let us engage that boat

to take us across." While crossing the river in it, they discovered

that it was a boat sent by the Demon of Blackwater River to entrap

them in midstream, and the Master would have been slain had not Sun and the Western Dragon come to the rescue.

The Slow-carts Country

Having crossed the Blackwater River, they journeyed westward,
facing wind and snow. Suddenly they heard a great shout of
ten thousand voices. The Master was alarmed, but Sun laughingly
went to investigate. Sitting on a cloud, he rose in the air, and
saw a city, outside of which there were thousands of priests and
carts laden with bricks and all kinds of building materials. This
was the city where Taoists were respected, and Buddhists were not
wanted. The Monkey, who appeared among the people as a Taoist, was
informed that the country was called the Ch'ê Ch'ih, 'Slow-carts
Country,' and for twenty years had been ruled by three Taoists who
could procure rain during times of drought. Their names were Tiger,
Deer, and Sheep. They could also command the wind, and change stones
into gold. The Monkey said to the two leading Taoists: "I wonder
if I shall be so fortunate as to see your Emperor?" They replied:
"We will see to that when we have attended to our business." The
Monkey inquired what business the priests could have. "In former

times," they said, "when our King ordered the Buddhists to pray for

rain, their prayers were not answered. Then the Taoists prayed, and

copious showers fell. Since then all the Buddhist priests have been

our slaves, and have to carry the building materials, as you see. We

must assign them their work, and then will come to you." Sun replied:

"Never mind; I am in search of an uncle of mine, from whom I have not

heard for many years. Perhaps he is here among your slaves." They said:

"You may see if you can find him."

Restraints on Freedom

Sun went to look for his uncle. Hearing this, many Buddhist priests

surrounded him, hoping to be recognized as his lost relative. After

a while, he smiled. They asked him the reason. He said: "Why do you

make no progress? Life is not meant for idleness." They said: "We

cannot do anything. We are oppressed." "What power have your

masters?" "By using their magic they can call up wind or rain." "That

is a small matter," said Sun. "What else can they do?" "They can make

the pills of immortality, and change stone into gold."

Sun said: "These are also small matters; many can do the same. How did
these Taoists deceive your King?" "The King attends their prayers night
and day, expecting thereby to attain immortality." "Why do you not
leave the place?" "It is impossible, for the King has ordered pictures
of us to be hung up everywhere. In all the numerous prefectures,
magistracies, and market-places in Slow-carts Country are pictures of
the Buddhist priests, and any official who catches a runaway priest
is promoted three degrees, while every non-official receives fifty
taels. The proclamation is signed by the King. So you see we are
helpless." Sun then said: "You might as well die and end it all."

Immortal for Suffering

They replied: "A great number have died. At one time we numbered
more than two thousand. But through deaths and suicides there now
remain only about five hundred. And we who remain cannot die. Ropes
cannot strangle us, swords cannot cut us; if we plunge into the
river we cannot sink; poison does not kill us." Sun said: "Then
you are fortunate, for you are all Immortals." "Alas!" said

they,

"we are immortal only for suffering. We get poor food. We have only

sand to sleep on. But in the night hours spirits appear to us and

tell us not to kill ourselves, for an Arhat will come from the East

to deliver us. With him, there is a disciple, the Great Holy One,

the Equal of Heaven, most powerful and tender-hearted. He will put

an end to these Taoists and pity us Buddhists."

The Saviour of the Buddhists

Inwardly Sun was glad that his fame had gone abroad. Returning to the

city, he met the two chief Taoists. They asked him if he had found

his relative. "Yes," he replied, "they are all my relatives!" They

smiled and said: "How is it that you have so many relatives?" Sun

said: "One hundred are my father's relatives, one hundred my mother's

relatives, and the remainder my adopted relatives. If you will let

all these priests depart with me, then I will enter the city with you;

otherwise, I will not enter." "You must be mad to speak to us in this

way. The priests were given us by the King. If you had asked for a

few only, we might have consented, but your request is

altogether

unreasonable." Sun then asked them three times if they would liberate

the priests. When they finally refused, he grew very angry, took his

magic spear from his ear, and brandished it in the air, when all their

heads fell off and rolled on the ground.

Anger of the Buddhist Priests

The Buddhist priests saw from a distance what had taken place,

and shouted: "Murder, murder! The Taoist superintendents are being

killed." They surrounded Sun, saying: "These priests are our masters;

they go to the temple without visiting the King and return home

without taking leave of the King. The King is the high priest. Why

have you killed his disciples? The Taoist chief priest will certainly

accuse us Buddhist priests of the murders. What are we to do? If we go

into the city with you they will make you pay for this with your life."

Sun laughed. "My friends," he said, "do not trouble yourselves over

this matter. I am not the Master of the Clouds, but the Great Holy

One, a disciple of the Holy Master from China, going to the Western

Paradise to fetch the sacred books, and have come to save

you."

"No, no," said they, "this cannot be, for we know him," Sun replied:

"Having never met him, how can you know him?" They replied: "We have

seen him in our dreams. The spirit of the planet Venus has described

him to us and warned us not to make a mistake." "What description did

he give?" asked Sun. They replied: "He has a hard head, bright eyes,

a round, hairy face without cheeks, sharp teeth, prominent mouth,

a hot temper, and is uglier than the Thunder-god. He has a rod of

iron, caused a disturbance in Heaven itself, but later repented,

and is coming with the Buddhist pilgrim to save mankind from

calamities and misery." With mixed feelings, Sun replied: "My friends,

no doubt you are right in saying I am not Sun. I am only his disciple,

who has come to learn how to carry out his plans. But," he added,

pointing with his hand, "is not that Sun coming yonder?" They all

looked in the direction in which he had pointed.

Sun bestows Talismans

Sun quickly changed himself from a Taoist priest and appeared in

his natural form. At this they all fell and worshipped him,

asking his forgiveness because their mortal eyes could not recognize

him. They then begged him to enter the city and compel the demons to

repent. Sun told them to follow him. He then went with them to a sandy

place, emptied two carts and smashed them into splinters, and threw

all the bricks, tiles, and timber into a heap, calling upon all the

priests to disperse. "Tomorrow," he said, "I am going to see the King,

and will destroy the Taoists!" Then they said: "Sir, we dare not go

any farther, lest they attempt to seize you and cause trouble." "Have

no fear," he replied; "but if you think so I will give you the charm to

protect you." He pulled out some hairs and gave one to each to hold

firmly on the third finger. "If anyone tries to seize you," he said,

"keep tight hold of it, call out 'Great Holy One, the Equal of Heaven,'

and I will at once come to your rescue, even though I will be ten thousand

miles away." Some of them tried the charm, and, sure enough, there

he was before them like the God of Thunder. In his hand, he held a

rod of iron, and he could keep ten thousand men and horses at bay.

The Magic Circle

It was now winter. The pilgrims were crossing a high mountain by

a narrow pass, and the Master was afraid of wild beasts. The three

disciples bade him fear not, as they were united, and were all good

men seeking truth. Being cold and hungry they rejoiced to see a fine

building ahead of them, but Sun said: "It is another devil's trap. I

will make a ring around you. Inside that, you will be safe. Do not wander

outside it. I will go and look for food." Sun returned with his bowl

full of rice but found that his companions had got tired of waiting,

and had disappeared. They had gone forward to the fine building, which

Pa-chieh entered. Not a soul was to be seen, but on going upstairs

he was terrified to see a human skeleton of immense size lying on

the floor. At this moment the Demon of the house descended on them,

bound the Master, and said: "We have been told that if we eat of your

flesh our white hair will become black again, and our lost teeth grow

anew." So he ordered the small devils who accompanied him to bind the

others. This they did and thrust the pilgrims into a cave,

and then

lay in wait for Sun. It was not long before the Monkey came up when

a great fight ensued. In the end, having failed, notwithstanding the

exercise of numerous magic arts, to release his companions, Sun betook

himself to the Spiritual Mountain and besought Ju Lai's aid. Eighteen

lohan were sent to help him against the Demon. When Sun renewed the

attack, the _lohan_ threw diamond dust into the air, which blinded the

Demon and also half-buried him. But, by skillful use of his magic coil,

he gathered up all the diamond dust and carried it back to his cave.

The _lohan_ then advised Sun to seek the aid of the Ancient of

Days. Accordingly, Sun ascended to the thirty-third Heaven, where

was the palace of the god. He there discovered that the Demon was

none other than one of the god's ox-spirits who had stolen the magic

coil. It was, in fact, the same coil with which Sun himself had at

last been subdued when he had rebelled against Heaven.

Help from Ju Lai

The Ancient of Days mounted a cloud and went with Sun to the cave. When

the Demon saw who had come he was terrified. The

Ancient of Days then
recited an incantation, and the Demon surrendered the magic coil
to him. On the recitation of a second incantation, all his strength
left him, and he appeared as a bull and was led away by a ring in
his nose. The Master and his disciples were then set at liberty
and proceeded on their journey.

The Fire-quenching Fan
    In the autumn the pilgrims found themselves in the Ssu Ha Li Country,
where everything was red--red walls, red tiles, and red varnish on doors
and furniture. Sixty _li_ from this place was the Flaming Mountain,
which lay on their road westward.
    An old man they met told them that it was possible to cross the
Flaming Mountain only if they had the Magic Iron Fan, which, waved
once, quenched the fire, waved a second time produced strong wind, and
waved a third time produced rain. This magic fan was kept by the
Iron-fan Princess in a cave on Ts'ui-yün Shan, 1500 _li_ distant. On
hearing this, Sun mounted a cloud, and in an instant was transported
to the cave. The Iron-fan Princess was one of the _lochas_ (wives

and daughters of demons), and the mother of the Red Child
Demon, who

had become a disciple of Kuan Yin. On seeing Sun she was
very angry,

and determined to be revenged for the outwitting of her
husband,

King Ox-head, and for the carrying away of her son. The
Monkey said:

"If you lend me the Iron Fan I will bring your son to see
you." In

answer, she struck him with a sword. They then fell to
fighting, the

contest lasting a long while, until at length, feeling her
strength

failing, the Princess took out the Iron Fan and waved it. The
wind

raised blew Sun to a distance of 84,000 _li_, a whirled him
about like a leaf in a whirlwind. But he soon returned,
reinforced

by further magic power lent him by the Buddhist saints.
The Princess,

however, deceived him by giving him a fan which increased
the flames

of the mountain instead of quenching them. Sun and his
friends had

to retreat more than 20 _li_, or they would have been
burned.

The local mountain gods now appeared, bringing
refreshments, and urging

the pilgrims to get the Fan to enable them to proceed on
their

journey. Sun pointed to his fan and said: "Is not this the
Fan?" They

smiled and said: "No, this is a false one which the Princess has

given you." They added: "Originally there was no Flaming Mountain, but

when you upset the furnace in Heaven five hundred years ago the fire

fell here and has been burning ever since. For not having taken more

care in Heaven, we have been set to guard it. The Demon-king Ox-head,

though he married the _locha_ Princess, deserted her some two years

ago for the only daughter of a fox-king. They live at Chi-lei Shan,

some three thousand _li_ from here. If you can get the true Iron

Fan through his help you will be able to extinguish the flames, take

your Master to the West, save the lives of many people around here,

and enable us to return to Heaven once more."

Sun at once mounted a cloud and was soon at Chi-lei Shan. There

he met the Fox princess, whom he upbraided and pursued back to

her cave. The Ox-demon came out and became very angry with Sun

for having frightened her. Sun asked him to return with him to the

locha Princess and persuade her to give him the Magic Fan, This he

refused to do. They then fought three battles, in all of which Sun was successful. He changed into the Ox-demon's shape and visited the

locha Princess. She, thinking he was the Ox-demon, gladly received

him, and finally gave him the Magic Fan; he then set out to return

to his Master.

The Power of the Magic Fan

The Ox-demon, following after Sun, saw him walking along, joyfully

carrying the Magic Fan on his shoulder. Now Sun had forgotten to ask

how to make it small, like an apricot leaf, as it was at first. The

Ox-demon changed himself into the form of Pa-chieh and went up to

Sun said: "Brother Sun, I am glad to see you back; I hope you have

succeeded." "Yes," replied Sun, and described his fights, and how he

had tricked the Ox-demon's wife into giving him the Fan. The seeming

Pa-chieh said: "You must be very tired after all your efforts; let

me carry the Magic Fan for you." As soon as he had got possession of

it he appeared in his true form, ad tried to use it to blow Sun away

84,000 _li_, for he did not know that the Great Holy One had swallowed

a wind-resisting pill, and was therefore immovable. He then put the

Magic Fan in his mouth and fought with his two swords. He was a match

for Sun in all the magic arts, but through the aid of Pa-chieh and

the help of the local gods sent by the Master the Monkey was able

to prevail against him. The Ox-demon changed himself many times into

several birds, but for each of these Sun changed himself into a

swifter and stronger one. The Ox-demon then changed himself into many

beasts, such as tigers, leopards, bears, elephants, and an ox 10,000

feet long. He then said to Sun, with a laugh: "What can you do to me

now?" Sun seized his rod of iron, and cried: "Grow!" He immediately

became 100,000 feet high, with eyes like the sun and moon. They fought

till the heavens and the earth shook with their onslaughts.

The defeat of the Ox-demon

The Ox-demon being of so fierce and terrible a nature, both Buddha

in Heaven and the Taoist Celestial Ruler sent down whole legions of

celebrated warriors to help the Master's servant. The Ox-demon tried

to escape in every direction, one after the other, but his efforts

were in vain. Finally defeated, he was made to promise himself and

his wife to give up their evil ways and to follow the holy

precepts
of the Buddhist doctrine.

The Magic Fan was given to Sun, who at once proceeded to test its

powers. When he waved it once the fires on Flaming Mountain died

out. When he waved it a second time a gentle breeze sprang up. When

he waved it a third time refreshing rain fell everywhere, and the

pilgrims proceeded on their way in comfort.

The Lovely Women

Having traveled over many mountains, the travelers came to a

village. The Master said: "You, my disciples, are always very kind,

taking round the begging bowl and getting food for me. Today I will

take the begging bowl myself." But Sun said: "That is not right; you

must let us, your disciples, do this for you." But the Master insisted.

When he reached the village, there was not a man to be seen, but only

some lovely women. He did not think that it was right for him to speak

to women. On the other hand, if he did not procure anything for their

meal, his disciples would make fun of him. So, after long hesitation,

he went forward and begged food of them. They invited him to their cave

home, and, having learned who he was, ordered food for him, but it was
all human flesh. The Master informed them that he was a vegetarian,
and rose to take his departure, but instead of letting him go they
surrounded and bound him, thinking that he would be a fine meal for
the next day.

An Awkward Predicament

Then seven of the women went out to bathe in a pool. There Sun, in
search of his Master, found them and would have killed them, only he
thought it was not right to kill women. So he changed himself into an
eagle and carried away their clothes to his nest. This so frightened
the women that they crouched in the pool and did not dare to come out.

But Pa-chieh, also in search of his Master, found the women bathing. He
changed himself into a fish, which the women tried to catch, chasing
him hither and thither around the pool. After a while, Pa-chieh leaped
out of the pool and, appearing in his true form, threatened the
women for having bound his Master. In their fright, the women fled to
a pavilion, round which they spun spiders' threads so thickly that

Pa-chieh became entangled and fell. They then escaped to their cave

and put on some clothes.

How the Master was Rescued

When Pa-chieh at length had disentangled himself from the webs, he saw

Sun and Sha Ho-Shang are approaching. Having learned what had happened,

they feared the women might do some injury to the Master, so they

ran to the cave to rescue him. On the way, they were beset by the

seven dwarf sons of the seven women, who transformed themselves into

a swarm of dragonflies, bees, and other insects. But Sun pulled out

some hairs and, changing them into seven different swarms of flying

insects, destroyed the hostile swarm, and the ground was covered a

foot deep with the dead bodies. On reaching the cave, the pilgrims

found it had been deserted by the women. They released the Master and made him promise never to beg for food again. Having given the

promise, he mounted his horse, and they proceeded on their journey.

The Spiders and the Extinguisher

When they had gone a short distance they perceived a great building of

fine architecture ahead of them. It proved to be a Taoist

temple. Sha

Ho-sShangsaid: "Let us enter, for Buddhism and Taoism teach the

same things. They differ only in their vestments." The Taoist abbot

received them with civility and ordered five cups of tea. Now he was

in league with the seven women, and when the servant had made the tea

they put poison in each cup. Sun, however, suspected a conspiracy

and did not drink his tea. Seeing that the rest had been poisoned, he

went and attacked the sisters, who transformed themselves into huge

spiders. They were able to spin ropes instead of webs with which to

bind their enemies. But Sun attacked and killed them all.

The Taoist abbot then showed himself in his true form, a demon with

a thousand eyes. He joined battle with Sun, and a terrible contest

ensued, the result being that the Demon succeeded in putting an

extinguisher on his enemy. This was a new trick that Sun did not

understand. However, after trying in vain to break out through the

top and sides, he began to bore downward, and, finding that the

extinguisher was not deep in the ground, he succeeded in effecting

his escape from below. But he feared that his Master and

the others

would die of the poison. At this juncture, while he was suffering

mental torture on their behalf, a Bodhisattva, Lady Pi Lan, came

to his rescue. With the aid of her magic, he broke the extinguisher,

gave his Master and fellow-disciples pills to counteract the poison,

and so rescued them.

Shaving a Whole City

The summer had now arrived. On the road, the pilgrims met an old

lady and a little boy. The old lady said: "You are priests; do not

go forward, for you are about to pass into the country known as the

A country that exterminates Religion. The inhabitants have vowed to

kill ten thousand priests. They have already slain that number all

but four noted ones whose arrival they expect; then their number will

be complete."

This old lady was Kuan Yin, with Shên Tsai (Steward), who had come to

give them a warning. Sun thereupon changed himself into a candle-moth

and flew into the city to examine for himself. He entered an inn

and heard the innkeeper warning his guests to look after their clothes and belongings when they went to sleep. In Travel safely through the city, Sun decided that they should all put on

turbans and clothing resembling that of the citizens. Perceiving

the innkeeper's warning that thieving was common, Sun stole some

clothing and turbans for his Master and comrades. Then they all came

to the inn at dusk, Sun representing himself as a horse dealer.

Fearing that in their sleep their turbans would fall off, and their

shaven heads are revealed, Sun arranged that they should sleep in a

cupboard, which he asked the landlady to lock.

During the night robbers came and carried the cupboard away, thinking

to find in it silver to buy horses. A watchman saw many men carrying

this cupboard, became suspicious, and called out to the soldiers. The

robbers ran away, leaving the cupboard in the open. The Master was very

angry with Sun for getting him into this danger. He feared that at

daylight they would be discovered and all be executed. But Sun said:

"Do not be alarmed; I will save you yet!" He changed himself into an

ant and escaped from the cupboard. Then he plucked out some hairs

and changed them into a thousand monkeys like himself.

To each, he
gave a razor and a charm for inducing sleep. When the King
and all
the officials and their wives had succumbed to this charm,
the monkeys
were to shave their heads.

On the morrow, there was a terrible commotion
throughout the city,
as all the leaders and their families found themselves
shaved like
Buddhists.

Thus the Master was saved again.

The Return to China

The pilgrims having overcome the predicted eighty
difficulties of
their outward journey, there remained only one to be
overcome on the
homeward way.

They were now returning upon a cloud that had been
placed at their
disposal, and which had been charged to bear them safely
home. But
alas! the cloud broke and precipitated them to the earth by
the side
of a wide river which they must cross. There were no
ferryboats or
rafts to be seen, so they were glad to avail themselves of the
kind
offices of a turtle, who offered to take them across on his
back. But
in midstream, the turtle reminded Hsüan Chuang of a
promise he had made

him when on his outward journey, namely, that he would intercede for
him before the Ruler of the West, and ask his Majesty to forgive all
past offenses and allow him to resume his humanity again. The turtle
asked him if he had remembered to keep his word. Hsüan Chuang replied:
"I remember our conversation, but I am sorry to say that under great
pressure I quite forgot to keep my promise." "Then," said the turtle,
"you are at liberty to dispense with my services." He then disappeared
beneath the water, leaving the pilgrims floundering in the stream with
their precious books. They swam the river, and with great difficulty
managed to save several volumes, which they dried in the sun.

The Travellers Honoured

The pilgrims reached the capital of their country without further
difficulty. As soon as they appeared in sight the whole population
became greatly excited, and cut down branches of willow-trees
went out to meet them. As a mark of special distinction the Emperor
sent his horse for Hsüan Chuang to ride on, and the pilgrims were
escorted with royal honors into the city, where the

Emperor and his
grateful Court was waiting to receive them. Hsüan
Chuang's queer
a trio of converts at first caused great amusement among
the crowds
who thronged to see them, but when they learned of Sun's
superhuman
achievements, and his brave defense of the Master, their
amusement
was changed into wondering admiration.

But the greatest honors were conferred upon the
travelers at
a meeting of the Immortals presided over by Mi-lo Fo, the
Coming
Buddha. Addressing Hsüan Chuang, the Buddha said, "In a
previous
existence you were one of my chief disciples. But for
disobedience
and for lightly esteeming the great teaching your soul was
imprisoned
in the Eastern Land. Now a memorial has been presented to
me stating
that you have obtained the True Classics of Salvation, thus,
by your
faithfulness, completing your meritorious labors. You are
appointed
to the high office of Controller of Sacrifices to his Supreme
Majesty
the Pearly Emperor."

Turning to Sun, the Buddha said, "You, Sun, for creating
a disturbance
in the palace of Heaven, were imprisoned beneath the
Mountain of

the Five Elements, until the fullness of Heaven's calamities, had
descended upon you, and yo